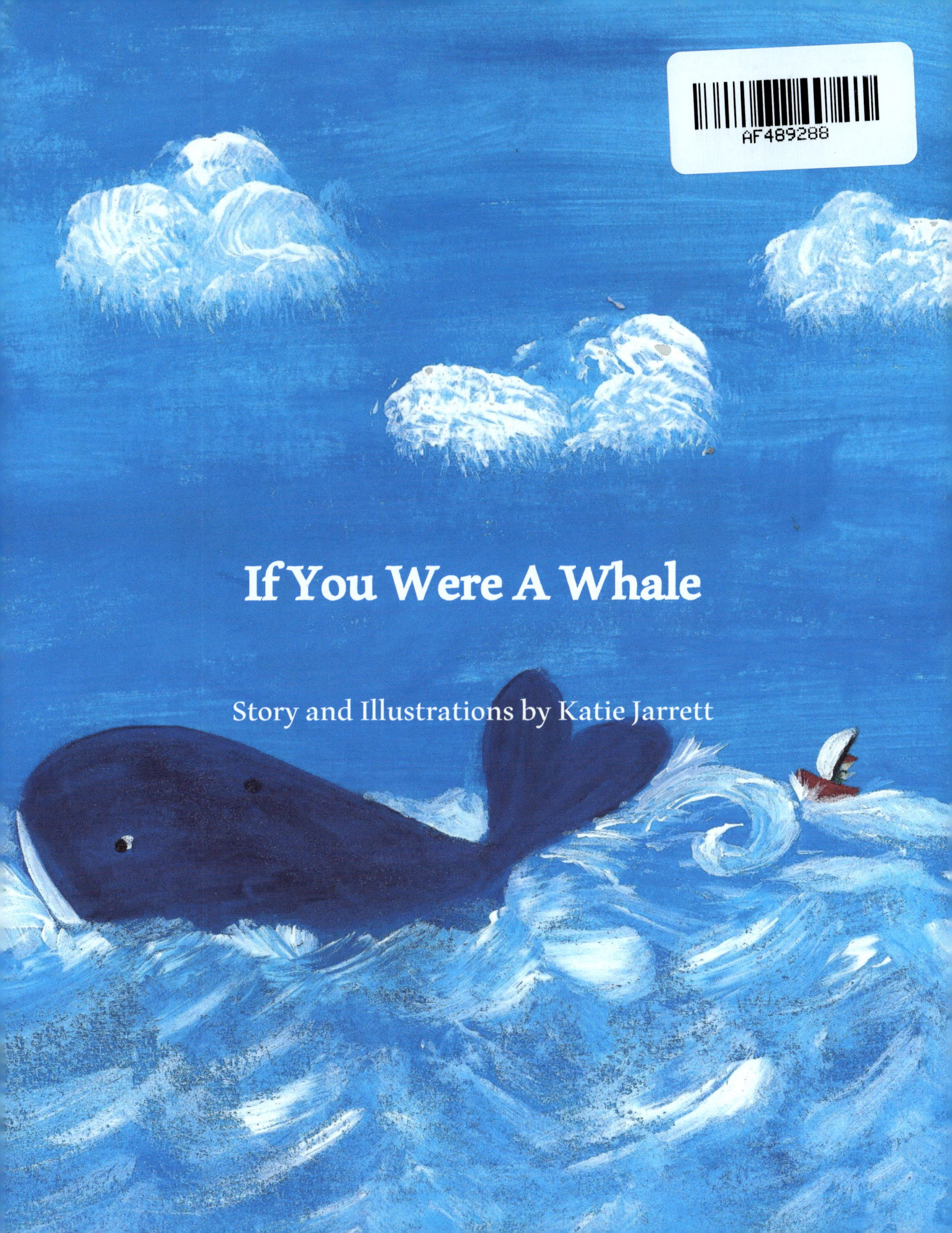

If You Were A Whale

Story and Illustrations by Katie Jarrett

AF489288

For Mom

Thank you for being the powerful force you are.

You have taught me to be strong and inspire me every day,

even at this time in your life. Love always.

If you were a whale in the deep blue sea,

would you come along my side?

And swim with me?

Would you dive deep in the ocean,

all the way down to the sand,

and swim back up quickly

because you are so grand?

A grand big whale

who moves water with each swim,

that can move a sailboat

even without any wind!

If you were a whale

would you swim fast or slow?

Would you dive far and deep,

then nap to catch up on your sleep?

Because as a big whale

you need your rest after the day.

All that swimming and diving,

all that very fun play.

Would you nap

in the ocean so grand,

so vast and big?

The ocean

that gives you soft sand to lay on,

that even lets you dig.

If you were a whale,

would you blow air through your spout?

After swimming deep in the ocean,

would you be so excited you would want to just shout?

Shout to your ocean friends

you swam so deep,

shout to your ocean friends,

you found a beautiful seashell to keep!

If you were a whale,

would you swim up to me in the deep ocean blue?

Would you stick by my side,

like a big heap of glue?

To make sure I am safe in this grand deep blue sea,

would you swim by my side even though you were free?

Free to roam the ocean wide,

free to roam the ocean side,

and hopefully meet up with me,

as I love swimming with you in the deep blue sea.

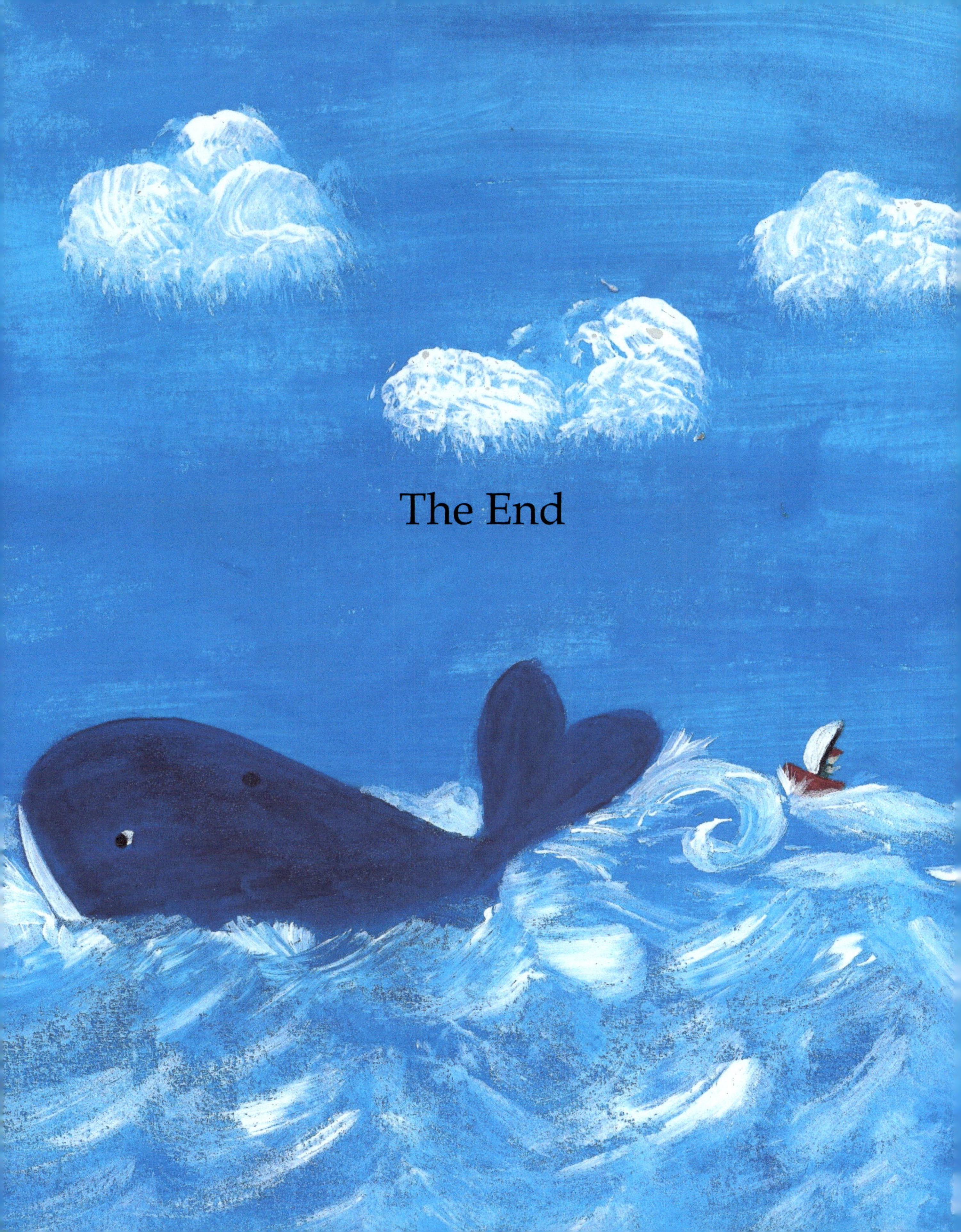
The End

About the author

My passion for reading and books started at an early age. I was born in Poland and immigrated with my parents and two sisters to America at the age of 5. Reading books and taking trips to the library became a part of our daily routine. Fortunate to have such great resources, I fell in love with books and the stories they told, and the feelings they stir up inside of us. Fast forward years later, my dream came true of writing and illustrating my very own books to share with the world. Thank you for taking the time to read

If You Were A Whale.

-Katie

StoriesByKatieJ.com

Other stories by Katie:

Good Morning Moon, Good Night Sun

The Secret Life of Golf Balls

If You Were A Dragonfly

If You Were A Giraffe

Christmas Time Is Almost Here

The Little Seed

Let's Go To Mars!

Poof the Scaredy Cat and the *Big* Thunderstorm

Did You Hear That?